LIGHT MAGIC

Books from OWL are published by Greey de Pencier Books,
56 The Esplanade, Suite 302, Toronto, Ontario M5E 1A7

*OWL and the Owl colophon are trademarks of the Young Naturalist Foundation.
Greey de Pencier Books is a licensed user of trademarks of the Young Naturalist Foundation.

Published simultaneously in the United States by Firefly Books (U.S.) Inc.,
P.O. Box 1338, Ellicott Station, Buffalo, NY 14205.

This book was published with the generous support of
the Ontario Ministry of Culture, Tourism and Recreation through the Ontario Publishing Centre,
the Ontario Arts Council and the Canada Council.

Canadian Cataloguing in Publication Data

Rising, Trudy L.
Light magic and other science activities about energy

Includes index.
ISBN 1-895688-15-9 (bound). - ISBN 1-895688-16-7 (pbk.)

1. Force and energy - Juvenile literature.
2. Power resources - Juvenile literature.
3. Force and energy - Experiments - Juvenile
literature. 4. Power resources - Experiments -
Juvenile literature. 5. Scientific recreations -
Juvenile literature. I. Williams, Peter, 1942-
II. Title.

QC73.4.R57 1994   j531'.6   C93-095371-1

For the purposes of this book, the word "battery" is used to apply to both dry cells and true batteries.

About the Authors
Trudy Rising and Peter Williams both have spent years sharing their love of science with children.
Trudy has taught at the junior high and high school levels, has written natural history books for children, and currently creates,
develops and publishes science educational resources. Peter is Assistant Science Co-ordinator for the Toronto Board of Education,
having had extensive experience teaching and writing about science for students, including developing
and co-authoring a major textbook series.

Acknowledgments
The authors would like to thank three fantastic teachers — Ann Heide, Carol Moult and Michael McLellan — for their help
early in this book's development, brainstorming activities; Professor Ernie McFarland for information on rainbows and air pressure; Jean Bullard for
the ball – glove idea on page 44; Professor Jim Rising for information on Australian brush turkey behavior; and Jane McNulty and Katherine Farris for their
excellent editorial work. Trudy also wishes to thank her son, John Rising, who designed some experiments and tested others, and Diane Klim,
who helped her write some. Peggy Williams is thanked by both authors for testing the activities in her grade 3 – 4 class. Lastly, the authors
wish to acknowledge the input of their children, students, friends and publisher — all the ideas they have provided over the years
have come together to form this introduction to energy.

Photo Credits
pp. 8 Foodland Ontario; 10 Bill Ivy; 12, 18, 28, 40, 45, 50, 60 Ray Boudreau; 14 Mike McQueen/Tony Stone Images; 16 (top) Bill Ivy; 16 (bottom) Alan Becker/
The Image Bank; 20 Morton Hovercraft, Bridgenorth, Ontario; 22 Red Huber/The Orlando Sentinel; 27 Satoshi Kuribayashi/Orion Press; 34 Industry, Science
and Technology Canada Photo; 38 Dick Haneda; 39 Larry Allan/The Image Bank; 42 Thomas Kitchen; 46 Vortek Industries Ltd.; 56 (top) National Research
Council Canada; 56 (bottom) Special Collections Division, University of Washington Libraries, Farquarson photo #4; 58 Odeillo Laboratory Group.

Design and art direction: Julia Naimska
Cover photography: Ray Boudreau

Printed in Hong Kong

A   B   C   D   E   F   G

LIGHT MAGIC

AND OTHER SCIENCE ACTIVITIES ABOUT ENERGY

**Trudy Rising
and Peter Williams**

illustrated by **Jane Kurisu**

Greey de Pencier Books

CONTENTS

INTRODUCING ENERGY

ENERGY, ENERGY, ENERGY! What is it? It's what makes things happen. You are full of it. Energy makes you move. Your home is full of it. It makes lights glow and refrigerators freeze; it makes water flow and fires burn bright. The world is full of it. It makes flags flap, flowers bloom, trees sprout leaves. Without energy, nothing happens. There's no light, no sound, no motion, no heat, no electricity. Nothing.

So energy is important. It's also amazing. Why? It comes in different forms...and it keeps changing form. Just when you think you've got it pinned down, zip...it changes. Each form of energy can change into all the other forms — light to electricity, electricity to sound, sound to motion, motion to heat. For example, when you plug in a kettle, you get electric energy changing to heat, to sound and to motion. When you eat breakfast, the chemical energy from the food is changed to heat to keep your body warm, and to motion when you run out the door. It's by changing forms that energy makes everything happen.

Take a close look at this picture. Can you find at least 10 ways that energy is making things happen? When you've finished this book see how many more you can spot!

6

STARTING WITH THE SUN

Has anybody ever told you "Sit still!" and you just couldn't? Your legs would swing, you'd squirm in your seat, your arms would twitch...know what your problem was? You were just too full of energy. Where did it come from? Indirectly it came from the sun.

The sun is a star. All stars in the universe produce energy, but the sun is special. Why? It's the only star that living things on Earth depend on for energy. What happens to that energy when it reaches Earth? Green plants, like trees, grasses, algae and some bacteria, capture the energy from the sun and store it.

The sun's energy is captured by the leaves of the apple tree and stored in the apple. When you eat the apple, the stored energy becomes your body's fuel.

What about the energy producing fuels we use, like coal, oil and gas? Where do they come from?

Many millions of years ago, the sun's energy helped tiny plants grow into forests that looked like this. Huge, tree-sized ferns, and other plants, grew beside shallow lakes.

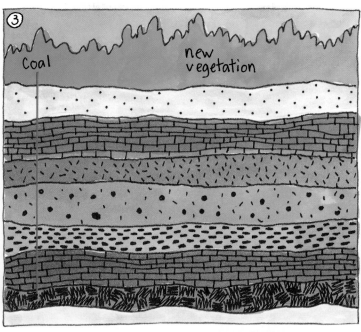

Millions of years passed and more layers of earth piled onto the forest layer. The pressure of these top layers squeezing downward caused the forest layer to change into coal.

Coal is called a fossil fuel. Oil and natural gas are fossil fuels too. They were formed much the same way as coal, except they were made from sea life instead of forest life.

Fossil fuels aren't much use lying deep in the earth. Why? Their energy is all stored up. If we want to use it, we need to transform it. How? By burning the fuel. Once it's burning, that stored energy can be used to heat our homes, generate electricity or run our cars.

That's what this book is all about: the different forms energy takes, the ways it can change, the ways we can use it. When you turn the page, you'll find experiments that let you change energy, store it, let it go, even use it for burning. You'll see that life and action depend on energy. Even if you manage to sit still while you read this book, energy is making things happen all around you and inside you. So use some of that energy and read on!

When the plants in the forest died, many fell into the water and sank. Since air couldn't get at them, they did not rot.

LIGHT FOR LIFE

O ur sun beams out huge amounts of energy all the time. How? The sun is a fiery hot ball of gas that keeps on exploding in nuclear reactions. These hot explosions produce solar energy that radiates into space.

Only a tiny fraction of the sun's energy reaches the Earth's surface. But what reaches us makes everything happen.

The word "solar" comes from the Latin word *solaris*, which means sun. Solar energy is energy that comes from the sun. This energy gives us light, keeps us warm and lets us live.

Solar Cells at Work

Solar cells use solar energy to power satellites and space labs. On Earth, they're used to supply power for buoys and unattended lighthouses, flashlights, watches and calculators.

Solar cells are made of silicon, which is found in sand. Each solar cell collects sunlight and changes it into electricity. One solar cell isn't very powerful, so lots of solar cells must be joined together in order to generate useful amounts of electricity.

Scientists are researching ways to set up solar cells in space to beam the sun's energy to Earth.

Why? Solar cells can receive 70 percent more solar energy if they are above the clouds in our atmosphere.

The sun may give us the answer to the problems of fossil fuels. Fossil fuels are non-renewable, and will get harder to find and more expensive until we finally use them up. They pollute the air as we burn them, and some harm the land and water if they spill or leak. Scientists are trying to find economical ways for us to depend more on solar power. Solar energy is free and clean. It doesn't pollute and it isn't dangerous to store. And it won't run out for millions of years.

FOCUS FILE

Solar Surprise

Collect just a few common objects, add sunshine, and watch the sun's energy cause something to happen.

What You'll Need

bright sunlight; newspaper; a few objects, such as kitchen utensils, a pencil, scissors, etc. (try to use different-shaped objects)

What To Do

1 Place the newspaper in direct sunlight.

2 Put several objects on the newspaper.

3 Leave the newspaper in the sun for several hours.

And Now

Watch what happens. Try some other kinds of paper to see if light will change their color. Then try leaving the paper in the sun for several days.

Dye Job

FOCUS FILE

Here's what happened. Wherever the sunlight hit the paper, it caused the paper to change color. Why? Solar energy causes the dyes that color newspaper ink and the paper itself to break down chemically. Presto! The dyes disappear because the chemicals have changed and all the color has been bleached out. Solar energy made it happen.

WHAT GOES UP...

Where does rain come from? It's made from the water in rivers, lakes and oceans. When that water gets heated up by the sun, it evaporates into the air. When the air cools, water begins to condense in the air, clouds form and rain falls on you.

But even though water evaporates and disappears, not everything in the water does. Huge deposits of salt have been found in dry land, far from any of today's oceans. How did they get there? The sea left them. Everything in the water was left behind when prehistoric inland seas slowly dried up and evaporated away.

To see how it worked, make a solar still and watch what happens when colored water is heated up by the sun's energy.

MAGIC FILTER

What You'll Need

a large clear container; a small yogurt container; marbles; plastic wrap; a rubber band; water with food coloring mixed in; a small stone

What To Do

1 Put the marbles into the yogurt container. Place this container inside the large container.

3 Stretch the plastic wrap tightly over the large container and secure it with a rubber band. Place the stone in the center of the plastic wrap. You've just made a solar still.

4 Place your solar still in a warm, sunny place.

And Now

Watch the changes that happen inside the still during the day.

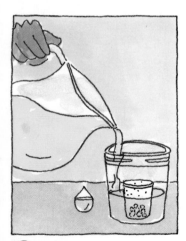

2 Carefully pour some of the colored water into the large container. Stop when it's about half-way up the side of the yogurt container.

A Drop to Drink

If you're ever camping and would like some extra water, make this special solar still.

Find a sunny spot, dig a hole, line the hole with plant leaves and put a cup in the hole.

Cover the hole with plastic wrap and wait a bit.

The sun's heat will make the water in the leaves evaporate. The vapor will condense (become a liquid again) on the plastic and the water droplets will fall into the cup. Only a little pure water can be collected this way. But it might be enough to wet your whistle.

COLOR IN YOUR LIFE

Quick! What are the two things you need in order to see a rainbow arch across the sky? Right. Sunlight and water. Solar energy gives us both these "ingredients." Sunlight is part of the energy we get from the sun, and water ends up in the sky as the sun evaporates it from lakes, rivers and streams (see page 12). Sunlight shines through droplets of water. The droplets break up the sun's white light into the separate colors we see in the rainbow.

Why Can You See a Rainbow?

FOCUS FILE

Next time it is raining in front of you and the sun is behind you, look up to a part of the sky that has a lot of water droplets in it. You might see a rainbow. Why? The light from the sun goes past you, hits the droplets, bends as it enters each droplet, bounces off the raindrop and comes back out towards you, bending once again. When the reflected light leaves the droplet and reaches your eye, it has been separated into the colors that make up white light. A rainbow is formed when you see the colors coming back to you from many, many droplets in the sky. And if the light bounces twice in each droplet? You see a double rainbow.

You don't have to look up to see rainbows. In the early morning you can see them when the sun shines on dew drops in the grass.

RAINBOW ROOM

Try making your own rainbow. All you need is sun, water and a little help from a mirror.

What You'll Need

a glass baking dish; a small mirror; water; a table; a window with a view of the sun

What To Do

1 Put the baking dish on a table top near a window that has a view of the sun.

2 Pour water into the dish until it is nearly full.

mirror

3 Put the mirror into the water so that the sunlight is reflected off it. Then move the mirror until the sunlight is reflected onto a white wall or ceiling.

> **!** *Don't look directly at the mirror reflecting the sunlight. Look instead at the wall or ceiling on which you're focusing the separated light.*

And Now

Look for the rainbow. The colors will always be in the same order. At one side, red, then orange, yellow, green, blue, indigo and, at the other side, violet.

Now You See It...

The rainbow you have created is called a color spectrum. This is the only part we can see of a larger spectrum known as the electromagnetic spectrum.

At either end of the visible part of the electromagnetic spectrum are two very important, but invisible, parts. Just beyond the red we can see, is the infrared (IR). Just beyond the violet we can see, is the ultraviolet (UV). The IR is the part that gives us the heat from the sun. The UV is the part that gives us the suntan from the sun.

Newspapers and television stations report a daily UV index to tell us when to avoid the sun so that we won't get burned.

UV Index

The forecast shows UV intensity in full sunlight at midday. The range is the average time in which a fair-skinned person will sunburn:

9 or higher — less than 15 minutes;

7 to 8.9 — about 20 minutes;

4 to 6.9 — about 30 minutes;

less than 4 — an hour or more.

FOCUS FILE

BLOW WIND, BLOW

Did you know the sun makes the wind? Here's how. When the sun shines it heats up an area of Earth. The air over the warm spot rises and cooler air moves in under it. Bingo! The moving air is wind. Wind can be mild or incredibly strong: its energy can bend trees, destroy homes and even flip small airplanes off runways. But in places where the wind blows constantly, people have found ways to put it to use. Instead of rows of crops, wind farms have rows of...yes, windmills! Modern windmills, like those shown below, have blades shaped like an airplane's wing that can swivel to use wind coming from any direction. The energy of the moving blades is used to generate electricity.

YOUR OWN WIND

Now's your chance to prove you can make hot air. How? Use the heat of your hands to make your own wind.

What You'll Need

paper and pencil; scissors; empty thread spool

What To Do

1 Trace the fan pattern onto your paper, then carefully cut it out.

2 Stick the eraser end of the pencil into the hole in the end of the spool.

3 Balance your fan on the pencil point. Be careful not to poke a hole in the paper fan.

4 Make sure your hands are warm. (If they're not, rub them together briskly.) Hold them, palms up, beneath the paper fan.

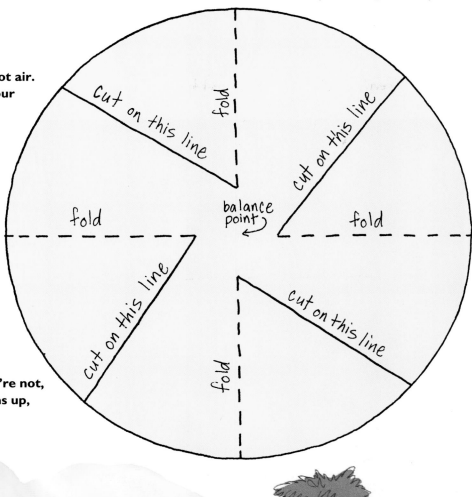

And Now

Watch what happens. Be careful not to touch the paper or the pencil. If your hands are warm enough, the fan will start to turn.

WILD WIND

You don't need to produce hot air to make a wind. You can just use your own energy. Exert some muscle power and watch it blow away.

STRING SHOT

Use your own energy to make a wild wind inside an empty plastic bottle.

What You'll Need

an empty plastic shampoo bottle; a piece of string (bottle-length or more); scissors

What To Do

1 Wash out an empty plastic shampoo bottle, just like the one shown here. Unscrew the cap.

2 Cut a bottle-length piece of string. Thread it through the small hole in the top of the bottle cap. Knot both ends of the string so that it can't slip through the hole. Put the string into the bottle and screw the cap back on.

3 With a sudden quick squeeze, press the sides of the bottle.

And Now

Watch what happens. Try changing the size of the bottle, or the length of the string, and see what happens

Cool Dogs

It may seem strange, but prairie dogs rely on wind in their underground homes. Why? Without the wind, there wouldn't be fresh air.

This prairie dog burrow has two holes to the surface. One hole is level with the ground. The other is surrounded by a small mound of earth. Air moves quickly over the mound and causes low air pressure at this exit. Air always moves from areas of high pressure to areas of low pressure. That means air above the first hole, where the air pressure is high, is forced through the burrow and out to where the pressure is low. This underground wind gives the prairie dogs plenty of fresh air!

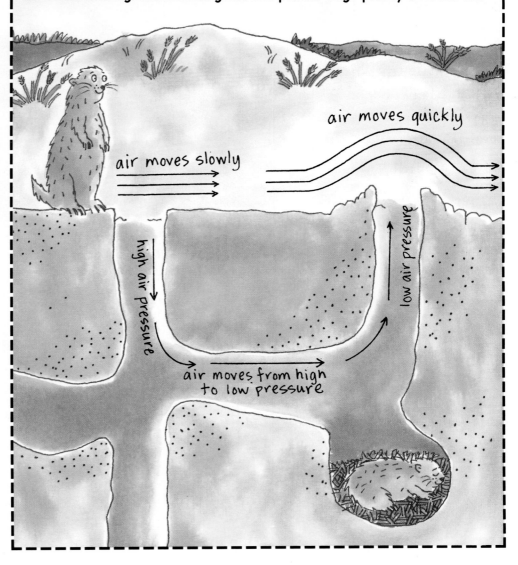

air moves slowly

air moves quickly

high air pressure

low air pressure

air moves from high to low pressure

RIDING ON AIR

An air-cushion vehicle (ACV) — or hovercraft — is a machine that moves across water or land on a "cushion" of air. How does it do it? Fuel burned in the ACV's engine makes a large fan spin. Air is blown by the fan down through the body of the ACV and is trapped underneath by a large rubber "skirt." The hovercraft rides on this trapped wind instead of on the surface of the land or water. Large ACVs can ride over waves up to 3 m (9 ft.) high and can go as fast as a car on the highway.

This two–person hovercraft goes about as fast as a car on a city street. Cushioned on 20 cm (about eight inches) of air, it skims over lakes, swamps, mudflats, snow and ice.

thrust air

lift air

What would it be like to drive your own personal ACV? With the engine off, your ACV floats like a boat. You turn the key to start the engine, and in seconds the craft rises off the surface on the "lift air" that forms the air cushion. Then the "thrust air" kicks in, blowing backward and propelling you forward — over water and right up onto dry land!

MAKE A MODEL HOVERCRAFT

Build your very own ACV that works on wind energy. Here's how.

What You'll Need

an empty thread spool; the lid of a plastic margarine container; scissors; glue; a balloon; a bowl, basin or tub of water

What To Do

2 Glue the spool to the top of the lid so that the two holes are lined up.

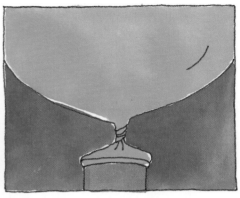

4 Pull the neck of the balloon over the spool.

5 Put your hovercraft down on the water. Let the balloon untwist so the air rushes out.

And Now

Your hovercraft should skim across the water. Try building other hovercrafts using different-sized balloons and different-sized plastic lids. When you've found the best combination, challenge a friend to a hovercraft race across water.

1 Carefully use the scissors to make a hole in the center of the lid. Make the hole the same size as the hole in the spool.

3 Blow up the balloon. Twist its neck to keep the air inside it, but don't tie a knot.

BLAST OFF!

How do you launch a rocket? Two chemicals — liquid hydrogen and liquid oxygen — get mixed in a special chamber. The result? A series of fiery hot explosions. The energy that is released during these huge explosions presses on the chamber walls and blasts out the rear. It forces the rocket up, up and away.

ROCKET CORN

You may not be able to launch a rocket, but you can get these popcorn kernels jumping, without using the stove.

What You'll Need

about 5 mL (1 tsp.) baking soda; measuring cup; about 60 g (1/4 cup) vinegar; about 250 g (1 cup) water; a shallow pan (a cake or pie tin will do); a few unpopped popcorn kernels; a tall drinking glass or jar

What To Do

❶ Put the glass in the shallow pan. Place several kernels of corn in the glass.

❷ Pour the water into the glass. Watch what happens.
• Pour the vinegar into the water. Watch again.
• Add the baking soda to the mixture. Do not stir.

And Now

Watch what happens. Can you get other things to "dance?" Try using rice, dried kidney beans and paper clips. Then do the same experiment but use table salt or sugar instead of baking soda. Do the same things happen?

It's a Gas

When you light a rocket's fuel or mix vinegar and baking soda, the same thing happens: you release chemical energy and new substances are formed. The gases formed by the rocket's engines push it upward into space. The gas bubbles formed by mixing vinegar and baking soda lift the popcorn kernels to the liquid's surface. When the bubbles burst, releasing the gas into the air, the popcorn kernels fall back down.

All things on Earth are made up of tiny, tiny particles held together by chemical bonds. When the bonds break apart and new ones form, energy — called chemical energy — is released. This is how cars and other vehicles get energy from the fuels they use. It's also how we get energy from food — food is our fuel.

FOCUS FILE

23

FOOD POWER

I nside this boy's body, a lot of action is going on — chemical action — to help him digest this apple. Here's what happens to his food.

The boy's teeth chomp it up into chunks. **Watery saliva dissolves the sugars, and enzymes start to break down some of the food into smaller and smaller bits. As these bits travel down into the stomach and then the small intestine, they meet chemical after chemical. Finally, they get turned into a mush of tiny bits of proteins, fats and sugars, along with minerals and vitamins.**

What happens to all these tiny bits of food?

In the small intestine, the food bits become so small they can move through microscopic holes in the intestine's walls and get picked up by the blood.

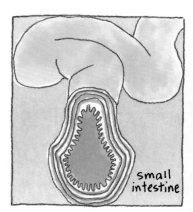

Bumps inside the small intestine are covered with tiny holes that food particles pass through.

The food is the body's fuel. The blood acts like a gas line, carrying it around the body to supply energy. The energy is used to make brain cells and muscle cells work; to build more blood and skin cells; and to make hair and fingernails grow.

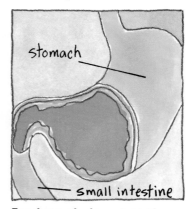

Food travels down into the stomach and then squeezes into the small intestine.

ROASTED NUTS

You've probably heard adults say, "I need to get some exercise to burn off that dessert I just ate." They aren't kidding. Your body uses the energy stored in food kind of like a wood stove uses wood. It burns it up. Not convinced food is a fuel? Try this experiment.

What You'll Need

half a roasted, shelled, unsalted peanut; a straight pin; a cork; a match; a watch or clock; a shallow pan or dish

What To Do

❶ Carefully poke one end of the pin through the peanut, then poke the other end of the pin into the cork.

❷ Place the cork on the pan. With an adult present, very carefully use the match to light the peanut. Blow out the match, and lay it on the pan.

❸ Time how long the peanut burns.

BREAKFAST OF CHAMPIONS

Jenny and Maria usually run neck-and-neck when they race. But one morning, as they ran home from school for lunch, Jenny won hands-down for the first time. Check the chart to see why.

	MARIA	JENNY
amount of sleep	8 hours	8 hours
food for breakfast	apple (one) 392 kJ	oatmeal (1 small bowl) 420 kJ
	milk (1 glass) 800 kJ	raisins (60 g / 1/4 cup) 340 kJ
		honey (30 mL / 2 tbsp.) 260 kJ
		milk (1 glass) 800 kJ

And Now

Repeat the experiment, but use a similar-sized piece of a different kind of nut. Whichever one burns longer gives you more energy.

Try other foods, such as a piece of marshmallow or a hunk of cereal.

A Joule Makes You Jump

Every bit of food you eat gives you energy. Some foods give you more energy, others less. There is enough chemical energy in an apple to keep you running for four minutes. When you eat, you cause an energy change — by using the energy from your food to move.

People used to measure the amount of energy in food in units called calories. But we now know that all forms of energy can be changed from one into the other. So all forms of energy are measured using the same unit. This unit is called the joule (J). (A kilojoule is equal to 1000 J.) How much energy is a joule? About the amount of energy it takes to pick up a baseball and raise it over your head.

LIGHT MAGIC

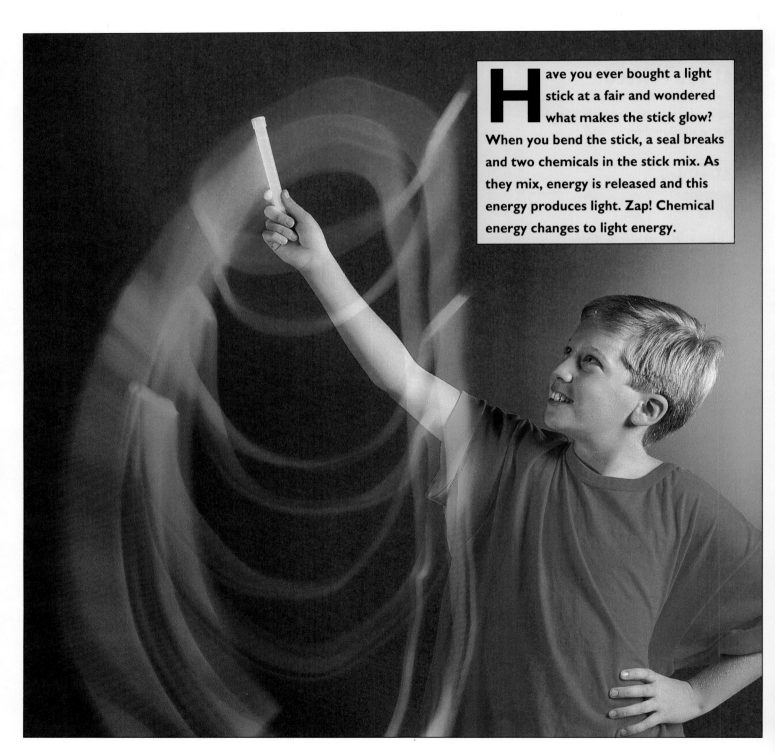

Have you ever bought a light stick at a fair and wondered what makes the stick glow? When you bend the stick, a seal breaks and two chemicals in the stick mix. As they mix, energy is released and this energy produces light. Zap! Chemical energy changes to light energy.

TURN ON THE LIGHT!

It's not quite so easy when you have to do it from scratch. Using the chemical energy of a dry cell (battery) and a combination of other things, try to turn on the light. Use only the batteries suggested.

What You'll Need

2 D-batteries or 2 AA-batteries; a flashlight bulb; plus any of the following: a plastic-covered wire [have an adult help you remove about 3 cm (about 1 in.) of plastic from around each end of the wire]; a strip of aluminum foil about 18 cm (about 7 in.) long and 3 cm (about 1 in.) wide, folded over twice along its length; paper clips; alligator clips; masking or electrical tape; a clothespin (spring type), and a piece of cardboard to make a bulb holder (see page 51)

What To Do

You choose. Use the batteries and any of the other things listed above. Your goal? To light up the bulb using the two batteries and your choice of objects. You can keep your design simple or make it elaborate.

And Now

Try out your design. Think about ways to improve it. (Here's a hint: what about a switch?)

The Inside Story

Very little happens inside a battery until someone connects a wire to opposite ends of the battery to complete a circuit. A circuit is a path for an electric current to flow through. The bulb lights up because energy from the chemicals in the battery is changed to electric energy once this circuit is completed.

Living Lights

Fireflies (shown below) blink their lights at one another all night long. How do they do it? They can change some of the chemical energy of their food into light. They aren't the only ones to put on a light show. Some deep-sea squids do it, so do glowworms in caves and so do tiny sea creatures called Noctaluca. When you dip a boat's oar into the water where they live, the water around the oar sparkles with light.

GOOD VIBRATIONS

Sound is a form of energy caused by vibrations. Vibrations are very quick movements back and forth. When you speak, the air from your lungs pushes against your vocal cords, making them vibrate. These vibrations create the sounds that you make. The vibrations leave your mouth and spread out in the air in the form of waves. When the sound waves push against the eardrums of other people, making their eardrums vibrate, the people can hear you.

"SEEING" SOUND

Create a soundscope to "see" the sound vibrations that your vocal cords make.

What You'll Need
a can with both ends removed; a round balloon; scissors; a rubber band; a piece of aluminum foil about 1 cm (about 0.5 in.) square; clear tape; a lamp with a 100 W bulb

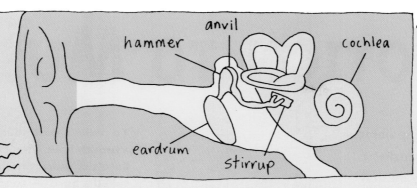

Your outer ear funnels some of these sound waves down your ear canal and into the eardrum. The sound waves make the eardrum vibrate.

This vibration makes the earbones vibrate. The earbones — called the hammer, the anvil and the stirrup — fit together in a way that makes the vibrations 20 times greater.

The vibrations then carry on into a snail-like part of the inner ear called the cochlea. It's filled with liquid. The vibrations make the liquid vibrate. The cochlea is lined with thousands of tiny "hairs" that are connected to nerve endings. The hairs detect the movements of the liquid and send the "sound" to the brain through a special nerve.

Your dad calls you to come to dinner. His calls send out sound waves into the air.

Your brain then makes sense of the sound, and you start running!

What To Do

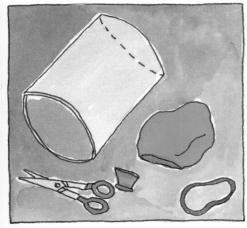

1 Blow up the balloon several times to stretch the rubber.

2 Cut off the neck and about 3 cm (about 1 in.) of the balloon.

3 Stretch the balloon over one end of the can. Hold it in place with a rubber band.

4 Lay the piece of aluminum foil shiny side up, on the balloon. Tape the foil to the center of the balloon.

5 Turn on the lamp in a darkened room. Hold the soundscope so that the aluminum foil reflects the light onto a wall or a ceiling.

6 Now talk into the open end of the soundscope.

And Now

Watch what happens to the reflected light. When it quivers, you're seeing the vibrations of your vocal cords. Different sounds look different. Try high sounds, low sounds, soft sounds, vowel sounds.

MOTION TO MUSIC

When something vibrates, that motion makes a sound. Every musical instrument vibrates in a different way to make its own unique sound.

Inside a piano are metal strings of various lengths and felt-covered hammers connected to the piano keys. When you play the keys, the hammers hit the metal strings, which vibrate. The sound-board underneath the strings also vibrates to make the sound you hear.

To make a flute sound, a player blows air across a mouth hole. This causes the air inside the flute's cylindrically-shaped wind passage — called a bore — to start vibrating.

A croaker is an instrument you can make (see page 31). The pull of your wet fingers causes vibrations in the string that are amplified by the cup. The bigger the cup, the greater the amplification.

A drum is made of a frame with skins stretched over it. When the skin is struck, the frame vibrates, amplifying the sound.

A guitar's sound is made when you pluck, pick or strum the six strings, causing them to vibrate. The vibrations are then reflected by the soundboard under-neath the strings.

CREATE A CROAKER

Here's your chance to make a truly original-sounding instrument. It's called a croaker, probably because it sounds like...well, you'll see.

What You'll Need

a small plastic yogurt container; scissors; a piece of string 45 cm (about 18 in.) long; a paper clip; a cup of water

What To Do

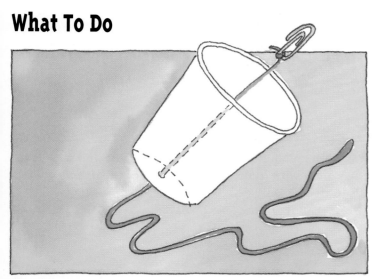

❶ Use scissors to make a small hole in the center of the bottom of the yogurt container. The hole should be just big enough for a piece of string to pass through.

❷ Tie the paper clip to the end of the string so that it won't slip through the hole. Thread the string through the hole.

❸ Hold the container in one hand. Dip the fingers of your other hand in the water to wet them. Then slide them down the string. Do this several times.

And Now

Listen for the sound. You'll find that the sound you can make improves with practice. Use different-sized containers to make more croakers, and compare the sounds they make. Get your friends to make croakers and compose a croaker concert. (If anybody is listening, they might want to use earplugs!) You can decorate your croaker any way you like.

FOCUS FILE

Sound Power

Even though you usually can't see sound, it can be incredibly powerful. A soprano singer, for example, generates a huge amount of energy bellowing one of her high notes. Sometimes the intense vibrations of her sound waves can shatter glass! And a rock group performing in a park recently caused people in nearby apartment buildings to think they were living though an earthquake. Why? The sound equipment generated inaudible vibrations that mimicked a tremor and caused the buildings to sway. Even tiny headphones can blare music loud enough to affect your ears. It's no wonder that one of every ten North Americans has some form of hearing loss. Avoid loud noises so that your ears serve you well for your whole life.

To check out the energy of the sound waves coming from the croakers, put a spoonful of rice into the containers. Watch what happens to the grains of rice when you pull on the string.

WIND AND WAVES

Everyone knows that wind can produce sound. But did you know that sound waves can produce wind? Sound fantastic? Try this experiment.

CANDLE SNUFFER

"Blow" out a candle without taking a breath. Sound impossible? Not when you make your very own Sound Wave Candle Snuffer.

What You'll Need
an empty, cylindrical plastic bottle; a balloon; a rubber band; scissors; a candle; a saucer; a match

What To Do

❶ Carefully use scissors to cut off the bottom end of the bottle. Then cut the balloon in half. Discard the half that has the neck.

❷ Stretch the other half over the bottle's cut end. Hold the balloon in place with the rubber band.

❸ With an adult present, light the candle and stick it to the saucer with molten wax. Careful of the dripping wax, it's hot!

❹ Hold the mouth of the bottle about 3 cm (about 1 in.) away from the candle flame. Flick a finger against the balloon.

And Now
Watch what happens to the flame. Then experiment to find out how to best position the bottle and flick on the balloon in order to snuff out the candle. Try different-sized plastic bottles to find out which ones make the very best candle snuffers.

Sound Levels

What's a decibel? a) a bell with 10 rings; b) the bell around a cow's neck; c) the unit used to measure the loudness of a sound.

If you guessed "c," you're right. The decibel (dB) is named after Alexander Graham Bell, the inventor of the telephone. Bell also taught the hearing-impaired. Check the following chart for the decibel levels of some common sounds and their effect on your ears. Where on the chart would you place the sound made by your candle snuffer? Check the answer at the bottom of the page to see how close you are.

COMMON SOUNDS	NOISE LEVEL (dB)	EFFECT
Jet engine (near)	140	Short-term exposure can cause immediate and permanent hearing loss
Jet takeoff	130	Threshold of pain (about 125 dB)
Thunderclap (near) Discotheque music	120	Threshold of sensation — you can feel the vibrations
Power saw Pneumatic drill Rock music band	110	Regular exposure of more than 1 min. risks permanent hearing loss
Garbage truck	100	No more than 15 min. unprotected exposure recommended
Subway Motorcycle Lawn mower	90	Very annoying
Electric razor Many industrial work places	85	Level at which hearing damage begins
Average city traffic noise	80	Intrusive, interferes with telephone conversation
Vacuum cleaner Hair dryer Noise inside a car	70	Annoying, interferes with conversation
Normal conversation	60	Comfortable
Quiet office Air conditioner	50	Comfortable
Whisper	30	Very quiet
Normal breathing	10	Just audible

Answer: We'd say about 40 dB.

33

FULL OF HOT AIR

Do you ever wonder how you might get a hot air balloon to float up and down? How would you launch it? And how would you get it back to Earth? Here's how. You make the balloon rise by warming up the air inside it. Then you make it descend by letting the air inside it cool down. Simple, isn't it? And it all works because of heat energy.

MOVING MONEY

Heat is the energy transferred from warm things to cold things. Use the heat from your own hands to make a quarter jump — without touching it!

What You'll Need

your hands; a little water; an empty juice or pop bottle (with a mouth about the size of a quarter); a 25¢ piece

What To Do

1 Rinse out the bottle with cold tap water.

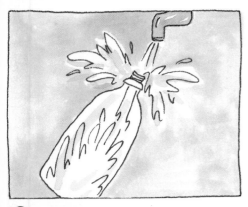

2 Moisten the mouth of the bottle. Moisten one side of the coin as well.

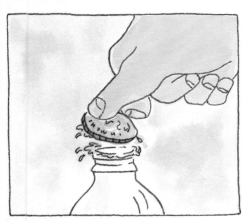

3 Place the coin wet-side down on the mouth of the bottle.

4 Rub your hands together briskly about 20 times until they tingle with warmth.

5 Tightly wrap your hands around the bottle.

And Now

Watch what happens to the quarter. Count the number of times you get the quarter to pop up. Try it again, but this time put the bottle in a freezer for half an hour. Then wet the bottle mouth and one side of the quarter and do the experiment again. Count the times it pops up.

Up, Up and Away

Everything on Earth — solid, liquid or gas — is made up of tiny, invisible particles that are constantly moving. When air is heated, its particles move faster and spread out. The air then occupies more space — it expands. When you rubbed your hands together, heat from your hands made the air inside the bottle expand. And that made the coin pop up. Hot air balloons float up for exactly the same reason. When the balloon is filled with hot air, it rises. When the air is cooled, the opposite happens. The air particles squeeze together and take up less space. The balloon then gradually deflates and descends back to Earth.

FOCUS FILE

HEAT UP, COOL DOWN

Hot air balloons and popping quarters show that warm air rises. So why isn't it warm on the top of a mountain? Here's why. Air is filled with tiny particles that bump each other. When they bump they create heat so the air warms up. As warm air expands and rises, the air particles start to spread out so they don't bump together as often. The less they bump, the cooler the air becomes. By the time the air reaches a high mountaintop, the particles are so spread out they hardly bump at all, and the temperature can be very cold.

In a hot air balloon, things work differently. The air particles can't spread out because they're trapped inside the balloon. And once they start to cool off, they get reheated by the balloonist.

−5°C (23°F)

10°C (50°F)

25°C (77°F)

YOU'RE IN HOT WATER

You've seen what happens to air that's heated — it expands and rises. Now see what happens to water when you heat it.

What You'll Need

a very small jar; a large jar (the small jar should fit easily into the large jar); water; food coloring; spoon; tongs or pliers

What To Do

1 Pour cold water into the large jar. Stop when it's about 3/4 full.

2 Fill the small jar with hot tap water. Quickly stir in about 10 drops of food coloring.

3 Using the tongs or pliers, carefully lower the small jar into the water in the large jar. Keep the small jar upright.

And Now

As soon as your apparatus is set up, watch what happens to the color of the water.

Hot on Top

Just like air, water expands when it's heated. The warmer, colored water spreads out and floats on top of the cooler water. That's why warm water floats at the surface of a swimming pool and the cooler water stays down toward the bottom of the pool.

FOCUS FILE

FEEL THE HEAT

If you touch a cold piece of fur and an equally cold piece of steel, only the steel feels cold to you. Why? Steel is a good conductor of heat, which means that heat travels through it very well. The reason a good heat conductor feels cold is that it removes heat from your skin. Fur is not a good conductor of heat. It's a good insulator.

Insulators are used to stop heat from being transferred from one object to another. They keep heat in — like a thermos — or out — like a picnic cooler. Air that is not moving is a very good insulator. And so are materials that trap air inside them, like fur, styrofoam and wool.

What does a warm coat do for you on a cold winter day? It traps your body heat and keeps it from being lost to the cold outside air.

This wolf's thick fur traps air and insulates against the cold. The wolf's white color provides good camouflage in the snow, but why is its nose black? Scientists speculate that where there is no fur to insulate, the black skin absorbs and holds heat from the sun, but they have no idea how to prove it!

Dead Heat

When old trees crash to the forest floor, the leaves and twigs become food for tiny bacteria. As the bacteria munch on their decaying lunch, they produce heat that some animals find useful.

Deep in the Australian rainforest lives a bird that relies on the heat of decaying leaf litter. As you can see, the Australian brush turkey looks a bit like a large black chicken with a bright yellow necklace.

The male brush turkey builds a huge mound of leaf litter. Then the female lays eggs in the mound. The male brush turkey scratches at the surrounding leaf litter, piling it higher and higher around the eggs. Neither the female nor the male sits on the eggs to keep them warm. Instead, they rely on the hungry bacteria in the leaf litter. As the bacteria feed, they produce heat that gets trapped in the mound. The heat helps the litter to decay and keeps the eggs warm. The eggs never get too hot or cold. Why? Because the male brush turkey just scrapes off some litter if he senses the mound is becoming too hot. And he piles more on if he senses it's becoming too cold. How does he sense this? You'll have to ask the brush turkey; no one else knows — yet.

BEAT THE HEAT

Here's the challenge: How long can you keep an ice cube from melting? Design your own ice-cube saver and see.

What You'll Need

an ice cube; a watch or clock; two containers (for example, small can, jar, paper or styrofoam cup, plastic bowl); any of the following: cotton; styrofoam chips; lint from a clothes dryer; plastic wrap to cover

What To Do

❶ Take two containers. Put one inside the other.

❷ Choose one of your insulators and put it between the containers.

❸ Take an ice cube and put it inside the inner container. Time how long it takes to melt.

And Now

Try it again. Change your design. Each time try a different material for the insulation. Which ones work best?

IN MOTION

Spectacular turns and twists — high speed — leaps in the air! This skateboarder is in motion! Where does he get the energy? He's fueled by the food that he eats. Motion can happen only if energy is stored first.

More fuel please.

POP-CAN ROLL

There are many ways to store energy and there are many ways to use it. This empty can rolls into motion on the energy stored in a wound-up elastic band. When you release that energy by letting the band go, you've changed the stored energy into the energy of motion. Z-o-o-o-o-m.

What You'll Need

an empty aluminum juice or pop can; thin cardboard; scissors; a rubber band (it's best to use a new one that isn't too big); a pencil; a small paper clip; a nail; a hammer; a large paper clip; a button; a round toothpick

What To Do

1 Cut a circle from the cardboard to fit inside the rim of the can. Use scissors to make a hole in the center of the cardboard.

2 Use the hammer and the nail to make a pea-sized hole in the center of the bottom of the can. Watch your fingers when you hammer!

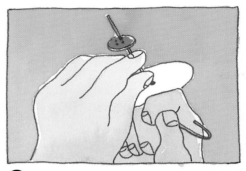

3 Straighten out one end of the small paper clip. Slip it through both the cardboard circle and the button.

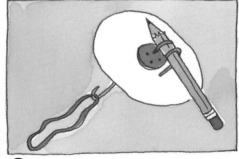

4 Twist the straight end of the small paper clip around the pencil. Hang the rubber band off the hooked end of the small paper clip.

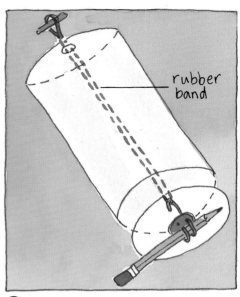

rubber band

5 Open up one end of the large paper clip to make a hook. Hook the rubber band with the clip and use the clip to pull the rubber band through the can, from the hole in the top to the hole you made in the bottom. When the rubber band pops through the hole in the bottom of the can, use the toothpick to anchor it.

And Now

Twist the pencil around to wind up the rubber band. When it feels tight, put the pop can on the floor and let it go. Try it on wood, tile and carpet to see on which surface it works best. (Turn the rubber band the same number of turns each time.) See if you can improve the can's performance by changing the length of the pencil, the thickness of the rubber band and the size of the can.

HOLD THAT MOTION!

This fast-flowing water is full of motion — and that means its energy can be used. How? The energy of the falling water can be harnessed to run turbines in an electrical generating station. But people can't always rely on waterfalls to keep electricity humming. Why? Waterfalls aren't found everywhere. What do people do when they don't have a waterfall? They dam up fast-flowing rivers and store the water in huge reservoirs. That way they can make their own waterfall. Whenever the energy is needed, the water is released. As the falling water turns the turbines, the stored energy of the water is changed into electric energy.

LET IT GO!

What You'll Need

a hammer; a small nail; a large can, (with a handle, if possible); twine or heavy string; scissors; a pitcher

What To Do

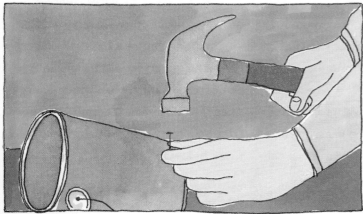

1 Use the hammer and nail to make four holes on one side of the can. The holes should be in a straight line near the bottom of the can, about 0.5 cm (about 1/4 in.) apart.

2 If the can has a handle, tie a piece of string to it. You'll be holding the can by this string. If the can does not have a handle, make one by hammering two more holes on opposite sides of the top of the can. Use scissors to cut a piece of string to make the handle. Thread one end of the string through one of the holes and tie it. Do the same with the other end of the string. When they are both secure, tie another piece of string to the handle you just made.

3 Go outside, or stand over a bathtub, and hold the can by the string with one hand. Pour water from the pitcher slowly into the can using your other hand. (Or do this with a friend so one of you can hold the can by the string and the other can pour the water.)

And Now

Watch what happens. Check which way the can moves.

Forward and Backward

FOCUS FILE

Water that flowed out of the can in one direction caused the can to move in the opposite direction. If there had been no holes, the energy of the water would have remained stored in the can. But the water was allowed to escape through the holes, so the water's energy was released and that made the can move. This experiment shows that for every action there is an equal and opposite reaction. The water flowed one way so the can moved the other way.

SLOWED MOTION

What's the one force that can slow motion? Did you guess friction? Right, friction is the force that fights movement between two surfaces. Sometimes it's a help for people in motion and sometimes it isn't.

Circus acrobats rely on friction to keep them aloft. They need just the right amount of friction between their feet and the high wire, or between their hands and the trapeze bar. You might notice that before they climb up, acrobats rub chalk or resin on their hands and feet. That's so that they can control their amounts of grip and slip!

But an ice skater wants as little friction as possible. The pressure of the skate blade on the ice melts a thin layer of water on the surface of the ice rink. Since the skater glides along on the thin layer of water, there's almost no friction to slow her down.

Imagine you're a baseball player making the perfect pitch right into the catcher's mitt. How much energy goes into throwing the ball? How does friction affect some of that energy? Look below to find out.

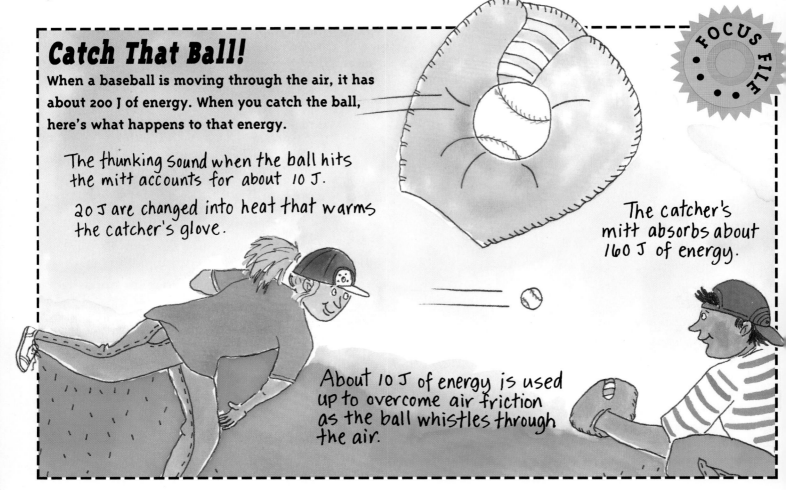

Catch That Ball!

When a baseball is moving through the air, it has about 200 J of energy. When you catch the ball, here's what happens to that energy.

The thunking sound when the ball hits the mitt accounts for about 10 J.

20 J are changed into heat that warms the catcher's glove.

The catcher's mitt absorbs about 160 J of energy.

About 10 J of energy is used up to overcome air friction as the ball whistles through the air.

FOCUS FILE

MAGIC BALL

Here's your chance to become a magician. Stop a sliding ball without even touching it. How? You put on the brakes by using friction to stop the slide.

What You'll Need

60 cm (2 ft.) aluminum foil scrunched into a ball; a sharp pencil; scissors; 60 cm (2 ft.) string; sticky tape; friends

What To Do

❶ Poke the pencil halfway through the scrunched up foil ball.

❷ Poke the pencil in again on the other side of the ball so that you've made a tunnel shaped like a wide "V" through the ball.

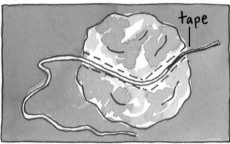

tape

❸ Wrap the tape around one end of the string to make it stiff. Then push the string through the hole.

❹ Hold the string straight up and down. The ball will start to slide downwards. Now pull hard on both ends of the string to make the ball stop. Practice a few times.

And Now

Ask your friends to call out "Stop!" and "Go!" When they yell "Go!" loosen your grip on the string. When they yell "Stop!" hold the string taut.

Put On the Brakes

Why does the ball stop? Because of friction. When the string is taut, it rubs against the edges of the holes and the corner in the center of the ball. The points where the string rubs the foil act as brakes by applying friction to the string.

FOCUS FILE

45

GLOWING LIGHTS

Look inside a clear light bulb at the thin metal coil. When you turn on the light, the electric current flows through this special thin wire and the wire begins to glow, lighting up the light. Why does the wire glow? The electric current makes the electrons inside the wire move. They bump into one another so often in this special wire that it heats up. The wire gets so hot it begins to glow.

Monster Lamp

Three scientists, Gary Albach, Dave Camm and Steve Richards, invented a huge lamp that gives off as much light as a 300 000 watt light bulb — bright enough to light 20 football fields! Called Vortek, the lamp can be used whenever intense light is needed, as this nighttime search and rescue demonstration shows. A light source this big also gives off enough heat to melt steel. So the inventors decided to think of it as a heat lamp, too. This idea really caught on. Vortek is used to test the heat shield on the space plane that will replace the shuttle. Scientists expose the plane to Vortek's heat to see if it can withstand the extremely high temperatures that occur when the plane re-enters Earth's atmosphere.

BUILD A BULB

Instead of buying a light bulb, can you make one of your own? Try this and see. Use only the batteries suggested.

What You'll Need

2 pieces of plastic-covered wire each about 45 cm (about 18 in.) long; a 6 V battery; 2 nails; a cork and an empty bottle for it to fit in; thin wire from steel wool

What To Do

❶ Push the nails through the cork. Attach the steel wool to the nail points.

❷ Fit the cork into the neck of the bottle with the nail heads outside and the steel wool inside.

❸ Ask an adult to help you remove about 3 cm (about 1 in.) of plastic from the ends of the two pieces of plastic-covered wire.

❹ Connect the wires to the battery and the head of the nails, as shown.

And Now

Watch what happens to the wire inside the bottle. How long does it glow before it falls apart?

A Waste of Energy

FOCUS FILE

If you put your hand near a lighted bulb, you can feel the heat coming from it. That heat is wasted energy. Only five percent of the energy used by ordinary light bulbs becomes light. The other 95 percent is changed to heat. Using a fluorescent bulb is a help. It uses 20 percent of its electric energy to make light. Less wasteful halogen bulbs are now available for you to use in your home, and even more efficient ones are being tested.

ELECTRIC EXCHANGE

Electricity doesn't just travel along wires. It can pass through a liquid, too. When it does, it can transform the metals in its path.

THE GREAT COVER UP

Amaze your friends. Turn a nickel green without using paint! Use only the batteries suggested.

What You'll Need

two pieces of plastic-covered wire, each about 30 cm (about 12 in.) long; a D- or AA- battery; scissors; a copper penny; a nickel; a short glass or jar; a box or a block of wood about the same height as the glass or jar; masking tape; vinegar; table salt; wooden spoon

What To Do

1 Ask an adult to help you remove about 3 cm (about 1 in.) of the plastic covering from the ends of the wires.

2 Tape each coin to a different wire. Make sure you leave some of the surface of each coin exposed.

3 Pour vinegar into the glass until it is about half full. Add about two tablespoons of salt and stir.

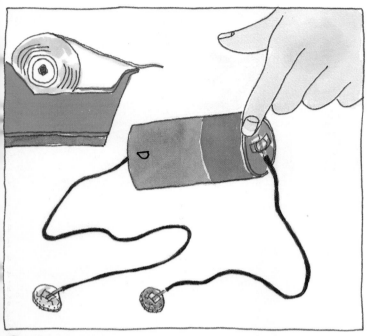

4 Tape the wire with the penny at the other end to the positive (+) pole of the battery. Tape the wire attached to the nickel to the negative (-) pole.

And Now

Watch what happens. Take out the coins and see how they have changed. Try these other cover-ups to see if a coating forms: a copper penny and a steel paper clip; a piece of aluminum foil and a copper penny. If you can't get them to work, switch the poles.

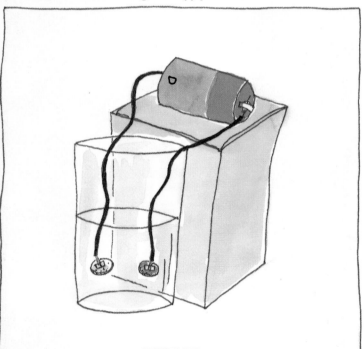

5 Put the battery on its side on the box or piece of wood so the coins don't quite touch the table. Drop the coins into the salty solution as shown. Make sure the coins don't touch each other.

FOCUS FILE

The Great Cover Up – Exposed

Want to know what you just did? You electroplated. It's a big word, but all it means is that you "plated," or "glued," one metal onto another. The bluish-green deposit you got on the nickel was mainly copper. How did you plate it onto the nickel? You completed an electric circuit through the liquid solution. As it passed through the solution, the electricity lifted some copper from the surface of the penny. The copper then combined with the vinegar and formed a coating on the surface of the nickel.

ELECTRIC DETECTIVE

This detective has almost solved the case. What was her mission? To find out what materials electricity will go through. These are the things that will "conduct" electricity.

Go with the Flow

You don't need to be a super sleuth to build this bulb holder and conductivity tester. Then you can use them to discover what electricity will flow through.

What You'll Need

a spring-type clothespin; masking tape; a flashlight bulb; a copper penny; a metal paper clip; 3 pieces of plastic-covered wire, each 45 cm (about 18 in.) long; a piece of cardboard (about twice the size of the clothespin); 6 V battery; 2 pencils with erasers; 2 unpainted metal thumbtacks

> **!** Use only flashlight or lantern batteries for activities on electricity. Never connect wires to an electrical outlet.

What To Do

1 Ask an adult to help you remove about 3 cm (about 1 in.) of plastic covering from the ends of three long pieces of plastic-covered copper wire. Twist one end of the first wire around the base of the bulb.

2 Clamp the clothespin around the twisted wire on the base of the bulb. Use several pieces of tape to fasten the clothespin to the cardboard, to make a bulb holder.

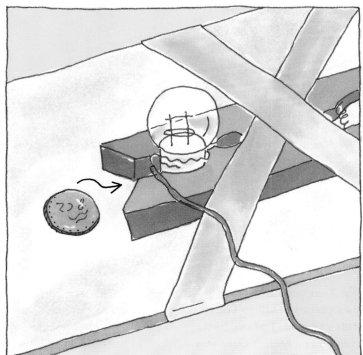

3 Slip the copper penny under the bulb and tape the edge of the penny down.

4 Attach one end of the second piece of wire to a paper clip. Slide the paper clip between the bulb and the penny so that the clip is touching both of them.

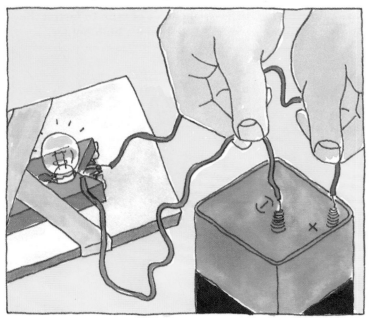

5 Test your design. Hold the free ends of each of the two pieces of wire. Touch them to the two opposite poles (+ and -) of the battery. If the bulb lights, everything's ready. If it does not light, try checking your wire connections at the bulb. If they are in place and the bulb still doesn't light, try a new battery.

Now make the rest of your conductivity tester:

6 Leave the twisted wire attached to the bulb and attach the other end of this wire to a battery pole. Attach the free end of the other wire and one end of the third wire to thumbtacks, and stick the thumbtacks into the pencil erasers.

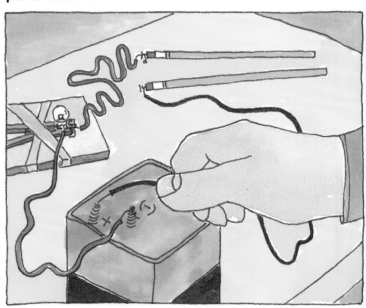

7 Next, attach the free end of the third wire to the opposite pole of the battery.

8 Test your conductivity tester by touching the tacks together. If the bulb lights, you're ready to start testing. If it does not light, check all your connections and try again until the bulb lights.

Shock Stoppers

Electricity travels well through some materials — copper, aluminum and other metals. These things are called conductors of electricity. Other things that don't conduct electricity — air, plastic and rubber — are called insulators. Because it is a good conductor, copper is used to make wires to carry electricity around our homes. Since they insulate, plastic and rubber are wrapped around those wires to protect us from dangerous electric shocks.

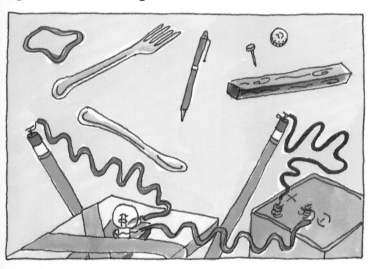

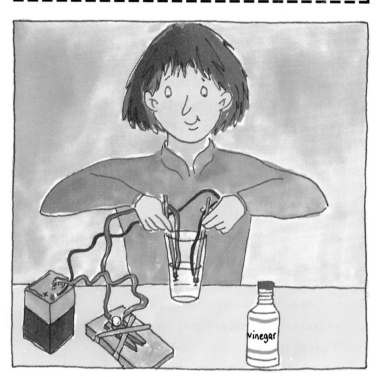

And Now

Start testing to find out what electricity will travel through. You already know it travels through thumb-tacks. You'll know what else works when your bulb lights up. Place both thumbtacks on an object, such as a metal fork, at some distance from each other. Did the bulb light up? Here are some things to try in place of the fork: a spoon, a quarter, an elastic band, a ballpoint pen, a piece of wood, a nail.

And now try this. Hold the pencils and place the thumb-tacks attached to them in a glass half-filled with vinegar. Don't let the tacks touch each other, and watch what happens.

THE INVENTION DIMENSION

What do you need to be an inventor? Lots of curiosity, no fear of making mistakes, a "wild mind" that lets you think about things differently, and lots and lots of patience.

Thomas Edison was one of the greatest inventors — we can thank him for the first phonograph in 1877 and the light bulb invented in 1878, among other things. Edison used a great combination of imaginative ideas and painstaking work. When he and his team were trying to design a glass bulb that would light, they experimented with more than 1600 different filaments, including hair from an assistant's beard, before they were successful. What did they finally use? Cotton thread. They found it would glow for up to 40 hours in their bulb. How long did it take them to make this discovery? Fourteen very long months! Edison was speaking from experience when he groaned, "Genius is one percent inspiration and 99 percent perspiration."

You probably won't perspire as you explore the three great inventions coming up on the next pages. But while you're working, maybe you'll think of — or stumble upon — a totally new invention or a different problem to solve. Perhaps you've got a wild idea already. If you do, be sure it's safe and then go for it, no matter how impossible — or crazy — it may seem. That's the way all great inventions get started.

Which invention do you want to try first?

A wind tunnel to help test aerodynamics? Go to *Blow It Away* on page 56.

A sure-fire way to cook a marshmallow — without a fire or an oven? Go to *Marshmallow Roast* on page 58.

A game board that lights up when players give you the correct answers? Go to *Bright Lights* on page 60.

BLOW IT AWAY

In 1903, the Wright brothers flew the world's first powered airplane. It took them years of research to get safely airborne. Why? Building and test-flying each of their ideas took a lot of time and effort. So to speed things up, in 1901 they built a wind tunnel to test how well objects will stand up to a wind. In just two months they tested over 200 models, figured out the best design, and then began building a full-scale airplane to test.

Wind tunnels are used today to test models of cars and bridges to see if they can stand up to strong winds. And Olympic skiers use them to figure out which crouch positions will help them go fastest.

Kelly Casey, a member of Canada's Olympic Ski Team, in a wind tunnel. As the air rushes past, a skier can check out which positions offer the least resistance to the wind.

Strong winds made this bridge buckle!

WHOOSH! IT'S A WIND TUNNEL

Build your very own wind tunnel and use it to test the design of your paper airplanes.

Tools of Invention

bottom half of a shoe box; plastic wrap; a hair dryer; paper; a paper clip; thread; a rubber band; a knife; scissors

What To Do

1 In one of the short sides of the shoe box, make a series of slits with the knife.

2 Cut a hole through the other short side of the box, just big enough to insert the nozzle of the hair dryer. Place the box on its long side.

3 Make a model of your favorite paper airplane to fit inside the box. Make a small hole in the top (long side) of the box at about the center. Knot one end of the thread around the paper clip. Slip the other end through the hole and tape it to the airplane. The plane should be suspended inside the box.

Let It Fly

Tightly cover the open part of the shoe box with plastic wrap and secure it with a large rubber band. Insert the nozzle of the hair dryer into the hole in the box. With an adult present, switch on a jet of air at the dryer's lowest (coolest) setting. If your plane is well designed, it will hang in the wind without too much wobble when the air hits it. Experiment with the shape and size of your plane, the direction of the plane in the tunnel and the speed of the wind. Make and fly larger versions of your most successful models.

MARSHMALLOW ROAST

The most powerful solar energy station in the world is in France. It has 63 flat mirrors that turn and tilt automatically to follow the sun. These mirrors reflect the sun's energy onto a larger mirror shaped in a special curve, called a parabola. The curve of the parabolic mirror concentrates energy coming from all 63 directions and reflects it onto a solar furnace, which heats up to 3 300°C (about 6 000°F). That's hot enough to melt most metals.

The station is used for developing different kinds of ceramics, "cooking" them at very high heats. But not all solar furnaces need to be this big or this hot to be useful. Solar cooking is something you can do, as you'll see when you try out this next invention.

Check out this high-tech energy producer in the French countryside. The mirrors are arranged in double rows — small ones in front of big ones — to catch as much sunlight as possible. Take a close look. Can you see the people in front of the solar furnace and the cars parked to the left of the parabolic mirror? This is one big oven!

SOLAR MARSHMALLOW MELT

To roast marshmallows you need a bonfire, right? Not necessarily. This solar cooker works by reflecting solar energy. Forget the fire. All you need is sunlight.

Tools of Invention

a shoe box; a clean 2 L (2 quart) plastic pop bottle; aluminum foil; a thin, unpainted metal clothes hanger; scissors; soap; pliers or wire cutter; lots of marshmallows

What To Do

1 Using scissors, carefully cut out half the bottle's middle.

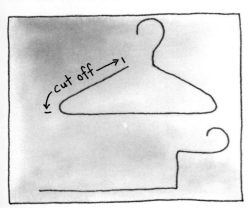

2 Open up the hanger. Ask an adult to help you cut off one end, as shown. Clean the hanger with soap and water. Bend the end with the hook into the shape of a handle.

3 Make a hole in the middle of the bottle cap. The hole should be just a bit bigger than the thickness of the hanger wire. Use the scissors to make a hole of the same size in the middle of the bottle's bottom.

4 Line the inside of the bottle with aluminum foil. Press the foil, shiny side up, tightly against the plastic.

5 Push the straight end of the hanger wire into the bottle, through the bottle cap end. Stick a marshmallow onto the clean wire.

6 Run the wire out through the bottom of the bottle. Place the bottle in the bottom half of the shoe box. Adjust the shoe box and the bottle so that they face the sun.

Taste Treat

Every once in a while, turn the wire handle so the sun's heat will melt the marshmallow evenly. When it's perfectly gooey and begins to brown, eat up!

BRIGHT LIGHTS

4.5 ÷ 3 + 4 =

34

(9 + 2) × 3 =

180

8 × 5 - 6

18

486 ÷ 27 =

33

1.8 × 100 =

Before you build your quiz board, here's a question to test your own brain power: What do twinkling lights at a fair, flashing lights on a billboard and timed city traffic lights all depend on? If you guessed electricity, you're right. To be even more specific, they all depend on electric circuits.

A circuit can be simple, like a bulb connected by wires to each pole of a battery — or complex, like the electrical systems that keep a large city's trains running smoothly. But they're all based on exactly the same idea: completing an electric circuit to make something happen.

Here's your chance to build five simple circuits and make some "bright lights" shine.

LIGHT BOARD

This electric quiz game is designed to challenge your friends. You'll need to invent five questions and answers to start. They can be on anything: your favorite sports, animals, math. You can use your game board over and over by changing the quiz questions.

Tools of Invention
10 bolts with nuts; a rectangular piece of cardboard 30 cm (about 12 in.) by 45 cm (about 18 in.); 5 plastic-covered wires 30 cm (12 in.) long [ask an adult to help you remove about 3 cm (about 1 in.) of the plastic covering from the ends of the wires]; a felt marker; labels; your conductivity tester from "Electric Detective," page 50

What To Do

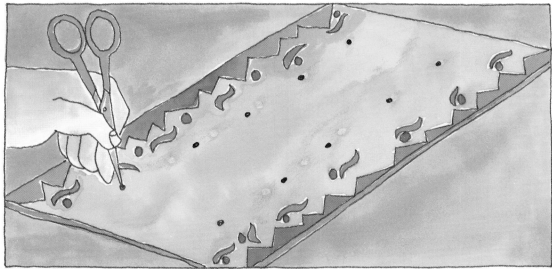

❶ Before you start to build your game board, decorate it using felt pens, crayons or colored pencils. To prepare your game board, make two rows each with five small holes running the length of the cardboard.

2 Beside one hole in the left row, stick on a label and write a question on it.

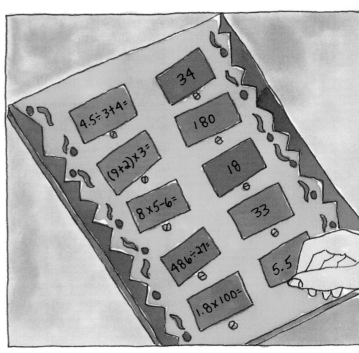

4 Place bolts through all the holes in both rows.

3 Write the answer to your question on another label beside one of the holes in the row on the right side of the cardboard. Do this for all the holes. Mix up the questions and answers.

5 Then turn the cardboard over. Wrap one end of a piece of plastic-covered wire around a bolt. Screw a nut onto the bolt to keep the wire secure.

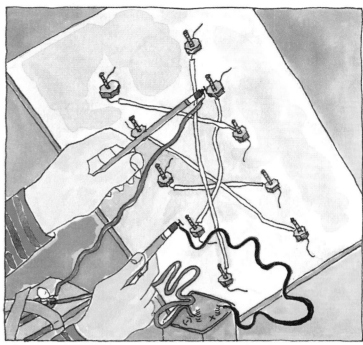

6 Then link the wire with the bolt attached to the right answer. Use another nut to secure this wire. Be careful not to tighten the nut too much. You might break through the cardboard.

7 Repeat this until all the matching holes are plugged with bolts connected by a piece of plastic-covered wire. Using your conductivity tester from "Electric Detective" (page 50), try out your gameboard to make sure that all the electrical connections are secure.

Try It Out

Now find out who are the bright lights among your family and friends. Use your conductivity tester from "Electric Detective" (page 50) to quiz the players. Ask the player to place the thumbtack stuck on one pencil eraser on a question. Then place the other tack on an answer. If the wires on the back match to complete a circuit, the bulb will light up. When all the questions have been answered, stick labels with new questions and answers over your old ones and start again.

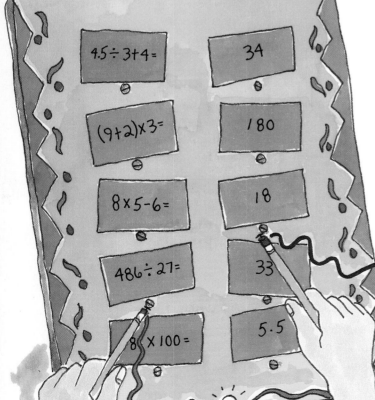

$4.5 \div 3 + 4 =$ 34

$(9 + 2) \times 3 =$ 180

$8 \times 5 - 6 =$ 18

$486 \div 27 =$ 33

$8 \times 100 =$ 5.5

INDEX

DATE DUE

FOLLETT